The
Broken Dozen
Mystery

Written by
Glen Robinson

Book 5
Created by
Jerry D. Thomas

Pacific Press Publishing Association
Boise, Idaho
Oshawa, Ontario, Canada

Edited by Jerry D. Thomas
Designed by Dennis Ferree
Cover art by Stephanie Britt
Illustrations by Mark Ford
Typeset in New Century Schoolbook 14/17

Robinson, Glen, 1953-
    The broken dozen mystery / written by Glen
Robinson ; created by Jerry D. Thomas.
        p.   cm.
    Summary: Sammy and the other Shoebox Kids learn
about helping others as they search for a missing painting from the Mill Valley Art Museum.
    ISBN 0-8163-1332-6 pbk. : alk. paper)
    [1. Mystery and detective stories.   2.   Artist.
3. Painting.   4. Christian life.] I. Thomas, Jerry D.,
1959- . II. Title
PZ7.R56616Br   1996
—dc20   96-15961
                                                        CIP
                                                         AC

96 97 98 99 00 • 5 4 3 2 1

Contents

Other Books in
The Shoebox Kids Series

Hi!

Do you like visiting museums? Have you ever been in a museum of children's art? What if your museum were showing a collection of paintings of children—and one of the pieces was mysteriously missing?

That's what happens to Sammy and Jenny in this new Shoebox Kids mystery!

The Broken Dozen Mystery is the third Shoebox Kids book written by my friend Glen Robinson. His story will pull you right into the mystery of a missing painting and a scary old woman in a rickety old house. Along the way, Sammy learns that helping others is part of what it means to be a Christian.

That's what the Shoebox Kids books are really all about—learning to be a Christian not just at church, but at home and at school. If you're trying to be a friend of Jesus', then the Shoebox Kids books are just what you're looking for!

Can you figure out what happened to the missing painting before Sammy and Jenny do?

Jerry D. Thomas

P.S. Book 6, *The Wedding Dress Disaster* is coming soon!

1

Mysterious Stranger

Sammy Tan discovered two things while standing on his head in the art gallery. First, that blood rushes to your head and it starts to hurt after a while. And second, that strange looking art still looks strange upside down.

Gradually, Sammy's body slid down from the wall he was leaning against. The world slowly turned right side up again. Sammy frowned and sat up, looking at the painting across the room. It still looked weird. Splotches of blue, green, and yellow covered wiggly black lines that ran from side to side.

"What are you doing, Sammy?" Sammy looked up from the floor to see Jenny Wallace walking toward him.

"Looking at sunspots," he answered.

"Sunspots? Where?" she asked. Sammy pointed toward the painting on the other wall as Jenny sat down on the floor next to Sammy.

"I can't figure why it's called 'Sunspots'," Sammy said.

Jenny looked at the painting silently. Then she said, "Well, have you ever looked at sunspots before? How do you know what they look like?"

"I've looked at an eclipse through special glasses," Sammy said. "I didn't see anything that was green or blue like that."

"Well, artists have a lot of imagination," Jenny explained, trying to defend the painting.

Sammy laughed and looked at the colorful splotches. "They must have to call something like that sunspots."

"What are you *doing* here?" Jenny asked him again. Sammy jumped up and walked over to a bronze sculpture of a woman with a hole in her stomach. He reached his arm through the sculpture and shook hands with himself.

"Right now I'm waiting for my grandfather," Sammy said. "He's taking a tour with some people in the other room. I'm supposed to wait for him here. We're going to see them open a new exhibit of some famous painter in the south wing—Sheply Matthews, or something." Sammy stood on his tiptoes and tried to put his head through the hole in the statue's stomach.

"I think that's Sheffield Matheson—the painter, that is." Jenny frowned at Sammy, who twisted his head as if it were stuck in the hole. "I don't think we're supposed to do that."

"Why else would they put a hole in her stomach?" Sammy asked. He sighed and pulled his head out of the hole. "What about you? Why are you here, Jenny Wallflower?"

"Don't call me that, Sam-*mule*," she emphasized the last part of his name. "My name is Wallace, and to answer your question, my mom is in charge of raising money for the new children's wing they're going to build here for the museum. She's in a meeting right now."

"Whoa, wait a minute," he said. "I know about bird wings. What's a children's wing?"

Jenny looked at him through the hole in the statue's stomach. "It's a neat place in a museum where they let you learn all about art, and feel things, and climb all over them." She looked at Sammy, who now had both of his arms in the statue's hole, and was trying to climb inside it. "Not that that's ever stopped you."

"Ahem." Sammy and Jenny heard someone clear his throat. Sammy climbed out of the hole quickly.

"Sorry, Grandfather," Sammy said, suddenly embarrassed. Jenny backed away, giggling.

"Sammy, art is for enjoying with the eyes, not with the hands, feet and elbows," Grandfather Tan said, wagging his finger in front of Sammy's face.

Sammy didn't have a chance to respond. A crowd of people followed Mr. Tan into the room, and Sammy realized that they were all headed to the south wing to see the exhibit opening. Sammy looked at all the faces, and saw Mrs. Wallace coming toward them. Sammy thought he saw someone else he recognized, but the person disappeared behind a group of others.

"Sammy! Mr. Tan!" Mrs. Wallace exclaimed. "It's good to see you!"

"Hi, Mrs. Wallace," Sammy said. "Jenny told me that you were in charge of raising money for the new children's wing here."

Mrs. Wallace smiled at Sammy, then looked at Mr. Tan. "That's right, Sammy. It's going to be a great place for kids to visit. And all kids, ages twelve and under, will get to come free anytime they want to."

"All right!" Sammy said, suddenly excited.

"How much money do you have to raise?" Mr. Tan asked.

Mrs. Wallace grew serious. "Seventy-five thousand dollars."

"Wow," Sammy said. "I can't even imagine that much money. I don't know anybody that has that much money."

Mrs. Wallace crouched down in front of Sammy. "You're right, it's a lot of money. But it's for a good cause. And if each of us do our part to raise it, I really think Mill Valley can afford to build this new wing." Mrs. Wallace squinted at Sammy and Jenny. "Say, how would the Shoebox Kids like to be involved in doing a little fund raising?"

Sammy and Jenny looked at each other. "How much do we get paid?" Sammy asked Jenny.

Jenny frowned. "The idea is to *raise* money,

not pay people like you. You're supposed to *volunteer*."

"Why don't we get the group together at our house this weekend?" Mrs. Wallace asked. "We can discuss the possibilities, have some snacks, maybe play a few games."

"Yeah, a regular party!" Jenny said.

"Well—OK," Sammy said finally.

Grandfather Tan, Sammy, Jenny and Mrs. Wallace heard a shout, and then applause. They looked up to see a man in a suit cut a ribbon, and then gesture for people to enter the doorway to the south wing. Sammy and the others joined the crowd and filed into a long room. Mounted on the walls on both sides were large paintings of children.

"I can't see," Jenny whispered. She stood on her tiptoes, trying to look through the crowd.

Sammy looked around, then tugged on her sleeve. "Come on."

Sammy led Jenny to a concrete bench standing right in the center of the room. They climbed onto the bench and stood up.

"Much better," Jenny said. "Wow, there must be a hundred people in here."

They looked around the room at the crowd. A

man up front was talking about the paintings.

"This is truly a historic occasion," the man said. "As director of the Mill Valley Art Museum, it is an honor for me to introduce this display of fine art to our city. But it is historic because this is the first time that all of Sheffield Matheson's works have been displayed at one place. It took a long time for me to arrange for this exhibit, but the fact that Sheffield Matheson was born, lived and died here in Mill Valley made a big difference. And the effort was well worth it."

Sammy looked around him at the paintings. All the pictures showed children. Sammy was fascinated by how the artist showed them. One showed three boys in a snowball fight, another showed girls painting a fence, one showed two girls swinging on a tire swing while boys in the tree above them yelled at them. Sammy could almost hear them talking. Then Sammy noticed that something was wrong.

"Excuse me!" he said out loud. "Mr. Director, I have a question."

"Sammy, don't interrupt," Grandfather Tan said quietly.

"No, it's all right," the director said. "What is it, son?"

Sammy pointed at the wall in front of him. "There are six paintings on that wall," he moved his hand to point at the opposite side, "and only five on that wall. How come?"

Jenny poked him in the ribs. "Because there's only eleven paintings, silly," she said.

"No, that's not quite right," the director said. "This set of paintings is called the Broken Dozen." He pointed at the far corner. "Sheffield Matheson wanted to paint children in each month of the year. But you'll notice that we have left a space between numbers ten and twelve over there. That's because number eleven disappeared in the fire that caused Mr. Matheson's death in 1964. It was actually just a few blocks from here."

"Well, didn't the painting just burn up in the fire?" someone else asked.

"Some think so, but the police who examined the fire say no. They said it would have left traces of the special fabric he painted on. And Sheffield Matheson was very careful to protect his paintings from fire." The director folded his hands over his chest. "It's just another unsolved mystery. In this case, it makes the work of Sheffield Matheson more interesting."

"Wow, a mystery!" Sammy nudged Jenny. "Wouldn't it be great if we could find that missing painting?"

"Yes! It would be like the treasure map Chris found, and the secret codes Willie got over his computer," Jenny answered. "Let's see if the director can give us any more clues."

Sammy listened to the director while he looked around the room. He had a strange sensation that someone was watching him. He scanned the paintings, then started looking around the room. A thin, gray-haired man on the far side of the room, dressed in an overcoat, turned and looked at Sammy. Sammy stared at him, thinking he should know him.

Sammy smiled at the man and waved. The man didn't smile back.

"Who is that man, Jenny?" Sammy whispered. "I feel like I should know him." Jenny looked past Sammy.

"What man?" Jenny whispered back.

"The gray-haired man in the raincoat," Sammy said. "Right over—." Sammy turned and pointed. But the man was gone.

2

Chasing Shadows

"I tell you, there was a man standing right over there," Sammy said to Jenny as the crowd began to file out. "He was creepy. He stared at me."

"What did he look like?"

"Sort of tall," Sammy raised his hand above his head to show Jenny. "He was wearing some sort of old raincoat. He looked like he had been sleeping in it. He had messed up gray hair."

Jenny shrugged. "It could have been any-body," she said. "Why don't we watch the exits and see who leaves the room?"

Sammy agreed. They stood on the concrete bench where they could see above the heads of the crowd. "Anything?" Sammy asked, as the crowd began to thin.

Jenny shook her head. The mystery man was gone. "If you don't know who it was, maybe he was here because of the paintings rather than because of you. You asked those dumb questions and he was probably drawn to you because of that."

"Dumb questions! At least they got us some valuable information about the mystery!" Sammy changed his tone. "What do you think? Is there a mystery for us to solve? Can we find that lost painting?"

Jenny shrugged again. "We won't know until we ask some questions." She looked over at the exit and saw her mother waving. "I've got to go. See you at the Shoebox this weekend."

Sammy looked around and finally saw his grandfather looking closely at the painting of the girls swinging in the tire swing. He walked over to him quietly, afraid to bother his grandfather while he was concentrating so hard. Finally, Grandfather looked up at Sammy, and his face broke into a smile.

"It always amazes me," Grandfather said, "that so much beauty can come from swabs of paint. Look closely, Sammy."

Sammy stepped close to the painting. "It's just different colored blobs of paint," he said.

"Yes," Grandfather said. "Blobs of paint. So simple. Now step back and look at it."

Sammy stepped back and the picture came into focus. The girls came alive as he saw them swinging in their tire swing. He could almost hear the boys laughing, hanging from the tree above them.

"Wow," Sammy said quietly.

"Come," Grandfather said. "I must get to the church. The afternoon is late, and I have agreed to mow the church lawn this week."

The two of them left the exhibit hall and headed outside.

"Grandfather," Sammy asked as they walked down the sidewalk to their car. "Do they pay you to mow the church lawn?"

Grandfather shook his head.

"Then why do you do it?" Sammy asked. "We have work to do at our house. Why can't someone else do it?"

"Sammy, can you name someone from our

church who doesn't have anything else to do?"

Sammy thought hard. "What about Mrs. Thomasson?"

Grandfather looked at him. "The old woman who comes to church in a wheelchair? Do you think she would be a good person to mow the lawn?"

Sammy shrugged. "I guess not. But I'm sure there are some people who aren't doing anything in church who could do this."

Grandfather nodded. "Sammy, you missed the point. I take turns mowing the church lawn because I wish to do this as a gift to God. The church is God's house. I want it to look as nice as possible. You know we put money in the offering plate at church. I think of my work as a different kind of offering."

Sammy thought as they walked to where their car was parked on the street. By the time they had fastened their seat belts and Grandfather had started the engine, Sammy had another question.

"What about those people who volunteer time for things that aren't at church?" Sammy asked. "Like Mrs. Wallace? She's taking her free time and helping the museum raise money for a children's wing. Why does she do that?"

Grandfather raised an eyebrow. "Why do you think, Sammy?"

Sammy frowned in thought for a long minute before answering. "Either because she likes art, or because she likes kids."

"Maybe she likes both," Grandfather said.

Sammy didn't respond. But he was thinking.

The usual gang gathered at the Shoebox that weekend. Jenny waited at the door for Sammy and handed him an envelope with his name on it.

"It's an invitation to my house tonight," Jenny said. "Mom's getting all the kids together to start raising money for the museum."

"Yeah, we can start figuring out how to find that missing painting when we get together," Sammy said.

"What missing painting?" Chris and Willie asked together.

"Do we have another mystery?" asked DeeDee and Maria.

"The party is to discuss fund raising for the museum, not solve any mystery," scolded Jenny.

"Class, it's time to get started," Mrs. Shue said.

"I'll tell you later," Sammy whispered to Chris and Willie, as he took his seat.

"Our lesson this week is found in Matthew 25, verses 31 to 40," said Mrs. Shue. "This is the story of the sheep and the goats."

"Sheep and goats!" Chris said. "I'll be a sheep. Baa!"

"I'll be a goat." Willie answered back with a deeper, "Baaa!"

"I'm not sure you want to be a goat in this lesson, Willie," Mrs. Shue said. "They don't get to go to heaven."

"No goats in heaven!" Willie responded.

Mrs. Shue shook her head. "That's not what I mean, Willie. I—just—." She let out a long sigh. "Would someone please volunteer to read the passage?" Maria raised her hand, and Mrs. Shue nodded gratefully.

Maria began to read: " 'When the Son of Man comes in his glory and all the angels with him, he will sit in state on his throne, with all the nations gathered before him. He will separate men into two groups, as a shepherd separates the sheep from the goats . . .' "

"Baa!" Chris bleated. Maria frowned at him. Chris shrugged. "Don't you like sound effects?" he asked.

Maria began again: ". . . and he will place the sheep on his right hand and the goats . . ."

"Baaaa!" Willie responded.

"Boys, please let her finish!" Mrs. Shue said with a smile.

". . . on his left. Then the king will say to those on his right hand, 'You have my Father's blessing; come, enter and possess the kingdom that has been ready for you since the world was made.

" 'For when I was hungry, you gave me food; when thirsty, you gave me drink; when I was a stranger you took me into your home, when naked you clothed me; when I was ill you came to my help, when in prison you visited me.'

"Then the righteous will reply, 'Lord when was it that we saw you hungry and fed you, or thirsty or gave you drink, a stranger and took you home, or naked and clothed you? When did we see you ill or in prison, and come to visit you?' And the king will answer, 'I tell you this: anything you did for one of my brothers here, however humble, you did for me.' "

The Shoebox was quiet for a long minute after Maria stopped reading. Then Chris spoke up. "So Christians are supposed to do good things for people, because one of them might be Jesus in disguise?" He looked at Mrs. Shue, who turned to the others.

"What do the rest of you think?"

Maria raised her hand. "I think we should do good things for people because we want to be like Jesus, and that's what Jesus would do."

Mrs. Shue nodded. "It all comes down to love. Do you love other people enough to help them when they need help? If you do, then you are doing what Jesus asks us to."

Willie raised his hand. "But Mrs. Shue, we can't bring strangers into our houses, or go and visit prisons. We're just kids. What can we do?"

"God has work for all of us to do," she said. "There are things you can do that no one else in the church can do. And helping someone— especially when it's your own idea— is usually far from boring. Think about it."

Sammy sat quietly and thought, *Is that why Grandfather works at the church like he does? If it is, what does Jesus want me to do?*

3

Is Anyone Home?

"So what's this about a missing painting?" Chris asked Sammy when the group got together that evening.

"There's this guy named Sheffield Matheson who is a real famous painter," explained Sammy. "And he lived right here in Mill Valley. Of course, this was in the olden days, back before computers or video games or color TV or stuff like that."

"It was in 1964," said Mrs. Wallace. "I was three years old."

"Wow! That long ago?" Chris said.

"Anyway, his paintings are worth about a zillion bucks each—"

"Not quite that much," Mrs. Wallace corrected.

"OK, not that much, but a lot," said Sammy. "And one of them is missing."

"What makes you think we can find it?" Willie asked. "When did they lose it?"

"They lost it in a fire in 1964." Sammy smiled and folded his arms over his chest. "Right here in Mill Valley."

"Oh, *right*," Chris said. "We'll be able to find this painting when the police and everybody else couldn't. How do we know it wasn't burned up in the fire?"

"Because the police said it wasn't," Sammy said.

"Even though we're meeting tonight to talk about raising money for the museum, somehow I knew this mystery would come up," Mrs. Wallace said, smiling. "I first got interested in art because my father collected everything he could about art history—especially things about local art and artists." She reached for a wide green scrapbook and opened it. "Here's a newspaper article that my father clipped several days after the fire."

The Shoebox Kids crowded around to look as Mrs. Wallace read from the old yellow paper. "Mill Valley police continue to investigate the fire that killed artist Sheffield Matheson and destroyed his studio at 1233 Jackson Street. Preliminary reports have concluded that the fire was most likely the result of arson."

"Arson—what's that?" asked DeeDee.

"That's when someone sets a fire on purpose," Mrs. Wallace said.

"But who would set fire to Mr. Matheson's studio?" Jenny asked.

Mrs. Wallace read on. "Mill Valley police are looking for Matheson's son, Berkeley, for questioning regarding the fire. Witnesses state that the relationship between father and son had been strained recently, and the two had been seen arguing violently in public on at least two occasions."

"Uh-oh," Willie murmured. Mrs. Wallace nodded, then read on.

"When asked if they thought the missing painting—number eleven in the just-completed Children's Dozen set—was taken by the son, police investigators had no comment."

"It doesn't look good for Berkeley," Chris said.

"Anyway, that's generally what the article says," Mrs. Wallace said, looking up. "If I remember right, Matheson had a daughter as well. Hmm." She flipped through the scrapbook some more. "Yes, here it is. Emily Matheson. She had just been married two weeks before the fire. And if I recall correctly, the marriage didn't last very long. I wonder what ever happened to her?" Mrs. Wallace looked off in the distance as if she were trying to remember something.

"I wonder if the house is still there," Willie asked.

"Oh, it's still there," Mrs. Wallace said cheerfully. "It was just the studio behind the house that burned down."

"Then maybe we should check it out tomorrow," Sammy said.

"Maybe you should," Mrs. Wallace said. "But remember that someone probably lives there, so don't go snooping around without permission. That's trespassing, and it's against the law."

"Now," she said, snapping the scrapbook shut and standing up. "We have snacks in the kitchen. Everybody get a plateful, and then let's sit down and talk about making some money for the museum."

"Mrs. Wallace, I suggest we raise money by collecting things for recycling," Willie said. "You know, aluminum cans, newspaper, scrap metal."

"Don't forget older sisters," Chris added. Maria glared at Chris.

"Willie, I think that's a good start," Mrs. Wallace said. "Let's make a list and see what other ideas we can come up with."

The evening ended about an hour later with the Shoebox Kids agreeing to meet at the Wallace's house the next morning. Jackson Street was just a few blocks over from the Wallace's, and Mrs. Wallace agreed to come check on them after they had had a chance to talk to whoever lived there.

The next morning, a line of bikes left a long trail through the orange and yellow leaves on the sidewalk. "Look," Willie called from out in front, "my chair leaves two trails!"

"Are you sure this is the place?" DeeDee asked quietly when they stood in front of 1233 Jackson Street.

Sammy nodded, pointing to the mailbox with

1233 painted in fading colors on the side.

"This place is spooky," Willie said, looking up at the big old house. The place looked like it hadn't been painted in twenty years. Windows were broken in the upstairs rooms, and an iron railing for the stairs leaned over to one side. The grass had grown impossibly high, and bushes and trees around the house looked as if they would swallow it whole.

"I don't think anyone lives here anymore," Maria said. "It looks abandoned."

Chris shook his head slowly. "No, someone lives here all right. It's Mrs. Sheckly. Remember her, Maria? She's the one who threw a pail of water on those kids who were trick or treating around here last Halloween."

Maria nodded slowly.

"This lady is *spooky*," Chris said. "She never talks to anyone on the street, and if you ever hear her say anything, it's because she's mumbling to herself." Chris lowered his head and rumbled under his breath.

No one said anything after that for a long while. Finally, Sammy got up his courage.

"Well, spooky or not, someone should go up to the door and see if she's home." He looked at the others, who in turn looked back at him.

"It's your mystery, Sammy," Willie said.

Sammy looked around him. "Jenny, you'll come with me, won't you?" he asked.

Jenny hesitated, then said, "Sure. We're in this together."

Although it was ten o'clock on a brisk fall morning, Jenny felt warm. *I'm just nervous,* she thought, and pulled off her sweater. She followed Sammy up the creaky front stairs while the other Shoebox Kids watched from the walkway in front of the house.

"Well, what now?" Sammy asked, as the two of them paused in front of the door. A big "No Salesmen" sign was tacked to the wall. Jenny noticed that the doorbell had been yanked out, and only bare wires showed in its place.

"I guess we knock," she said, shrugging her shoulders.

Sammy pulled the screen door open and knocked once quietly. After a few seconds, he tried again, more loudly. No answer.

"I guess no one is home," Sammy said to the others.

"Maybe Mrs. Sheckly is out back," Chris said. He peered down the gravel driveway, then bent down to put up the kickstand on his bike.

"Chris, Mrs. Wallace said not to trespass," Maria said.

"I'm not going to trespass," Chris said as he walked down the driveway. "I'm just going to see if she's in her backyard." Chris disappeared around the corner of the house. After a few seconds, they heard him call.

"Hey guys, come look at this!"

"I'm not so sure about this," Jenny said, as the others disappeared down the driveway and around the corner of the house. "Sammy," she added with a quivering voice. "Let's stay up here and wait for them to come back."

"I'm sure they're all right," Sammy said. "After all, they just went around the—"

Sammy was interrupted by a scream from DeeDee. A second later, Willie, Chris, DeeDee and Maria came charging back down the driveway.

"What was it?" Sammy asked.

No one answered. Chris, Maria and DeeDee jumped on their bikes and started down the street after Willie, who had a head start on them. Realizing they were being left behind, Jenny and Sammy ran to their bikes.

"What *was* it?" Sammy yelled after them.

4

Meeting Mrs. Sheckly

"Wait, you guys!"

Finally, the others listened and slowed down to stop on the next block. Sammy and Jenny stopped right behind them. "What did you guys see back there?" Sammy asked. "A rhinoceros or something?"

DeeDee was still trying to catch her breath. Between gasps, she tried to tell what happened. "I heard Chris yell for us to come, and so I went with the rest of them up the gravel driveway."

"You think the front is overgrown," Willie added. "The back yard is a regular jungle."

"Yeah, a person could go in there and disappear for the rest of their life," Chris said.

DeeDee went on. "Anyway, Chris was trying to show us this bush—some sort of rosebush—that grew against the back of the house. It must have been fifteen feet tall."

"Twenty," Willie said. "It climbed all the way up the back of the house."

"Well, what scared you?"

"A *man!*" DeeDee almost screamed. "While we were looking at the rosebush, a man came right out of the bush at the bottom, and stared at us."

"It must have been some hidden door at the base of the bush," said Willie. "I guess we didn't see it. It could have been painted green."

"I guess it wasn't such a good idea to go back there," Chris said.

"At least without permission," Maria said. "I told you."

"Tell me about the man," Sammy said quietly. "What did he do?"

"Nothing, really." Willie scratched his head. "He just kind of stared at us."

"He scared me," DeeDee said. "It was a strange place, and I wasn't expecting any man to pop out of a rosebush in front of me—"

"What did he look like?" Sammy asked.

"He was tall and thin, and he had a long raincoat on," Maria said.

"Did he have gray hair?" Jenny asked.

"Yes. And it was messy." Maria said. "He could have used a haircut."

"He looked creepy, and it was a creepy place," DeeDee said. "I'm going home."

"I'll go back to the Wallace's with you, DeeDee," Chris said.

"I think we all should head home," Maria said. Everybody nodded and started to get on their bikes again.

"Wait," Jenny suddenly said. "I forgot my sweater!"

"Jenny!" Chris moaned.

"I think—no, I *know* I left it on the front porch. I laid it on the railing." Jenny looked at the others, who suddenly wanted to go back to a familiar house. "Oh, you guys go on. It will just take me a second to ride back and get it."

"I'll go back with Jenny," Sammy said.

Jenny and Sammy didn't expect the house to be as creepy the second time they saw it, but somehow it was. Clouds had covered up the sun, and the darkness of the midday made Jenny and Sammy uncomfortable as they rode up to the walkway in front of the house.

"Where did you leave your sweater?" Sammy whispered to Jenny. Once again they crept up the rickety wooden stairs to the front door.

"Right over—it's gone!" Jenny said. She looked both ways on the wide porch. "I thought I hung it on the handrail right there, but, but— it's not there!" Sammy saw that Jenny was about to cry.

"Don't worry, Jenny. We'll think of something," he said. Sammy looked around the porch. Dead leaves lay in deep piles on the porch. He noticed a window a few feet away, covered with dirt.

Sammy heard Jenny inhale suddenly and he turned toward her. Her eyes were as wide as saucers. She tilted her head toward some thick bushes at the far end of the porch. Sammy saw wide yellow eyes staring at him out of the darkness. Then he heard a low howl, and he laughed.

"It's just a cat, silly," he said. "Relax."

Sammy quietly walked over to the window

and pressed his face up to one of the panes. He pulled it away, and Jenny saw that the dirt from the window was now on his face. Sammy took the sleeve of his coat and rubbed away a patch of dirt on the window.

"There," he said. "Now we can see what's going on inside."

Jenny joined him and peered into what looked like the living room. The furniture looked like it had been there for a long time. Wallpaper was peeling off the walls. A worn rug spotted with stains lay on the floor.

"Look there," Jenny whispered, pointing. Across the room from them was an old, beat-up couch. Lying across the back of the couch was Jenny's sweater.

"What now?" Sammy asked.

"Well, we can knock again," Jenny said. "Maybe we'll have better luck this time."

"I don't know," Sammy said. "Maybe we should go get your mom."

"Let me try it just once," Jenny said. "Then we can go get mom."

Sammy took a deep breath, then nodded. Jenny walked over to the front door and knocked.

"Hello," she said to the door. "Mrs. Sheckly.

Are you there?" Jenny knocked for a couple of minutes, with no success.

"Well, let's head back," Sammy said.

Jenny started to answer when she heard a muffled woman's voice come from above them. Jenny and Sammy looked at each other, and Jenny walked over to the far end of the porch. She leaned over the railing to look up at the window where the noise had come from.

"Jenny, be careful," Sammy said. "Those boards don't look too sturdy over there."

"Just a second, Sa—" Jenny's words were swallowed up as her foot crashed through the boards beneath her.

"Jenny!" Sammy yelled, and rushed to help her. But when he got close, the boards began to make cracking sound under his feet.

"Sammy, stay back!" Jenny shouted. She stood on one foot, while the other disappeared into the floor up to her knee. Another board creaked beneath her.

"Can you get out? Are you hurt?" Sammy yelled back.

"I think I can get my foot out," Jenny said, fighting back tears. "But it hurts! The boards cut my leg." She sat back on the floor behind her.

Crying silently, she pulled her leg out of the hole. Sammy winced at the long red scratches that ran down her leg. A trickle of blood ran from one.

"Who's out there?" Sammy and Jenny heard a woman's voice. "If it's you teenage hoodlums again, I'll call the police!" The screen door opened a crack, and Jenny and Sammy looked at each other.

"Come on!" Sammy said.

"I can't!" Jenny said. "Run for it, Sammy! Run and get Mom!"

Sammy looked at Jenny sitting on the broken porch. Then he looked at the dark figure coming out of the door. Sammy heard thunder boom above them, and he lost his courage. Sammy leaped over the edge of the porch into the bushes.

Crouching in the bushes beneath the porch, Sammy watched as the old lady came through the door and walked across the porch. Jenny sat beside the broken boards, quietly sobbing. She watched as Mrs. Sheckly slowly walked up to her and looked at both her and the broken boards.

"Who are you?" Mrs. Sheckly almost shouted.

"What do you want?"

Jenny looked scared to death, but she squeaked out a reply. "I'm—I'm sorry I broke your porch," she said.

Sammy watched from the bushes, still unsure of what to do. Mrs. Sheckly hobbled closer to Jenny, then stopped. Her voice suddenly grew soft.

"Are you OK?" Mrs. Sheckly said to her. "Of course, you're not all right. You're hurt." She looked down at Jenny as if trying to decide what to do.

"Well, I can't carry you. Lord knows I have a hard enough time getting around myself. But you need something to help stop that bleeding. Do you think you can walk?"

Jenny nodded, and the old lady reached a feeble hand down to help Jenny back up to her feet. "I'm sorry I broke your porch," Jenny said again.

"Oh, don't worry about that old thing. The termites ruined it a long time before you stepped on it." The two of them leaned against each other as they walked slowly across the porch, and into the front door.

Sammy sat there for a long time, trying to

decide what to do. *Hiding in the bushes isn't helping anyone*, he thought. *Should I run for help, like Jenny asked me to? Or should I follow her into Mrs. Sheckly's living room?*

5

Sneak Attack!

Thunder rolled across the sky again. Sammy crouched under the bushes beneath Mrs. Sheckly's front porch. After several long minutes, he stood up. "I have to know what's going on with Jenny," he mumbled as he quietly climbed back onto the porch. As quietly as possible, he crept toward the dirty window of the living room.

"Hello, Mrs. Wallace?" Mrs. Sheckly said into the old phone. "My name is Mrs. Sheckly. I live over on Jackson Street." She paused. "Twelve thirty-three, that's right. I have a little girl here who has injured her leg."

Jenny lay on the couch with her leg propped up on a pillow. As she listened, she noticed an old family Bible laying next to the couch. *It's beautiful*, she thought. Carefully, she lifted the heavy old Bible and placed it in her lap. It had a heavy cover with gold-colored metal trim around the edges. She opened it carefully, and the pages opened to the book of Micah.

"No, I don't think it's that bad," she heard Mrs. Sheckly say to the telephone, "but I don't think she would want to ride her bicycle home." Pause. "Well, maybe it's best that she explain what happened when you come over to pick her up."

"Once more thou wilt show us tender affection and wash out our guilt," Jenny read, "casting all our sins into the *depths* of the sea." Jenny noticed that the word *depths* was underlined.

Mrs. Sheckly hung up the phone and smiled over her thick glasses at Jenny. "Your mom will be over in just a few minutes," Mrs. Sheckly explained. "Your friends' parents have just arrived and she's seeing them off. Now," and Jenny noticed that her voice had turned serious. "You need to explain to me why you and your friends were sneaking around my house."

Jenny gulped. How much of the mystery should she share with Mrs. Sheckly? Finally she thought, *Why not all of it?*

"My friend Sammy and I were at the art museum last week and we saw the paintings by Sheffield Matheson that were there," she explained. Jenny watched for Mrs. Sheckly's reaction, but the lady acted as if she had never heard the name.

"They have this set of paintings called the Broken Dozen," Jenny continued. "The man there said that the last painting in the set— number eleven—was in Mr. Matheson's studio when it burned down. And my mom told us that he used to live here."

"So you thought you would come over here and look for the lost painting," Mrs. Sheckly said. "Didn't your parents ever tell you about private property, and that it's against the law to trespass?"

Jenny nodded her head soberly.

"I've had too many problems caused by thoughtless teenagers on my property." Mrs. Sheckly's voice softened. "I don't get around very well since my eyes aren't working so well anymore. Maybe that's why I seem so mean to kids." Then she shook her head and looked at Jenny. "Yes, Sheffield Matheson lived in this house many years ago. I know the story, but looking around here is a waste of time. There's no painting. If there were a painting, I would have found it a long time ago."

"All that's left is this house and Sheffield Matheson's family Bible," Mrs. Sheckly added, pointing to the big book in Jenny's lap.

Jenny looked down. "This is his Bible? Wow!" She stared at the page it was opened to and noticed that three other verses were written next to Micah 7:19. *Why would Sheffield Matheson write those other verses in here?* She quickly tried to memorize them: Deuteronomy 5:8; Romans 15:20; and Revelation 20:1.

Outside the window, Sammy watched Jenny and Mrs. Sheckly talking. After a while, he realized that Jenny was in no danger. He heard a noise behind him and saw Mrs. Wallace's car drive up in front of the house.

Jenny and Mrs. Sheckly were still talking when they heard a knocking at the door. "Just a minute." Jenny watched Mrs. Sheckly hobble across the floor to the front door. Outside the door stood Mrs. Wallace and Sammy.

"Hi, Mom," Jenny said weakly when the door opened. Sammy waved shyly from behind her.

"Jenny!" Mrs. Wallace said. "Are you all right?" She rushed across the room and knelt by Jenny to check her leg.

"I'm afraid she's the victim of a termite-eaten porch," Mrs. Sheckly said, chuckling. "I don't think she's hurt too bad. I've cleaned her scratches up already."

"I'm so sorry this happened, Mrs. Sheckly." Mrs. Wallace said.

"I'm not," Mrs. Sheckly responded. "I mean, I'm sorry she hurt her leg, but I'm glad I got the chance to meet Jenny." She nodded toward Jenny. "Just don't be a stranger now, Jenny."

"I promise I'll come back," Jenny said, as Sammy and Mrs. Wallace helped her out the door to the car.

"I'm sorry I ran away, Jenny," Sammy said, sitting by her later in the Wallace's living room.

"That's OK, Sammy," Jenny said. "It turned out all right."

"What was Mrs. Sheckly like?" DeeDee asked.

4—B.D.M.

"Were you scared?" Chris asked. Chris, DeeDee and the other Shoebox Kids had come back to Jenny's house when they heard that she had been injured.

"I was at first," Jenny admitted. "She yelled at me when she first came out. But then I found out that kids in the neighborhood have been tearing up her yard. She can't get around very well, so she tries to scare them to keep them away. Actually, she's just lonely." Jenny was quiet for a moment. "She asked me to come back and see her. And I will."

"What about the mystery?" Chris asked. "Are we ever going to find the painting?"

"She didn't think there was a painting," Jenny said. "Besides, people are more important than solving a mystery."

"Her place really needs cleaning," Maria said. "We should offer to wash her windows."

"And rake her leaves," Chris added.

"And fix her porch," Jenny said.

"I'm not sure I want to hear her yelling at us," DeeDee said.

"Hey, guys," Sammy said, suddenly excited. "What if we sneak over there while she's gone, and rake her yard? She'll come back and be excited that someone has done something good for her for a change. But the fun part will be that she won't know who did it."

"Great!" said Chris. "A sneak attack to clean up! But how do we know the neighbors won't call the police while we're there?"

"I can call the Mill Valley police beforehand," Mrs. Wallace said, who was just entering the room. "I think when I explain what we're doing and why, they'll be understanding."

"Fine," Jenny said. "Then let's plan on this Friday after school. She told me that her neighbor takes her to the grocery store every Friday afternoon. We'll watch for them to leave, then move in and clean up the yard." She looked up at Mrs. Wallace. "We promise we won't go anywhere we're not supposed to."

Is that clock broken? Sammy thought for the fourth time Friday afternoon. *Will school ever end?* He heard a loud sigh from Jenny and knew she was thinking the same thing.

Finally, the bell rang and everyone headed to Jenny's house. Willie, who went to a different school, was already there when they arrived. Willie's dad brought their van, filled with rakes and a large supply of plastic bags. Mr. Wallace had left his pickup with Jenny's mom. She had her work clothes on and was loading a box full of window washing equipment when the kids showed up.

"Everything's all set," Mrs. Wallace said. "I let the police know, and they were very understanding. I even called the neighbor who takes her and found out that they always leave at three o'clock. I told her about the secret clean up, and she promised to keep it a surprise."

"Oh great, now the whole world knows who we are," Chris said.

"Relax, Chris," Maria said. "We just don't want any trouble."

The Shoebox Kids, Mr. Teller, and Mrs. Wallace piled into the van and pickup and drove over to Jackson Street a few minutes before three. Before long, Mrs. Sheckly's neighbor drove up and a few minutes later, Mrs. Sheckly was loaded into the car and they were gone.

"OK, everybody out," Mr. Teller yelled as they pulled up in front of Mrs. Sheckly's house. "Grab a bag and a rake, and let's get going."

"Maria, Jenny, do you want to help me on the windows?" Mrs. Wallace said as she pulled the box of cleaning supplies from the pickup.

"How long will they be gone?" Willie asked.

"About forty-five minutes, so we have to work fast," said Mrs. Wallace. She and the two girls with her had already started spraying and wiping the windows.

"I'll keep a special look out for their car," Willie said. He pulled his rake toward him across the brown leaves.

Isn't this great, Sammy thought. *She'll be so happy to see her yard cleaned up.* He paused and looked up from his raking. A movement across the street caught his eye. *Is that a person standing under that tree? Could it be . . .* He closed his eyes and shook his head. When he opened his eyes again, no one was there.

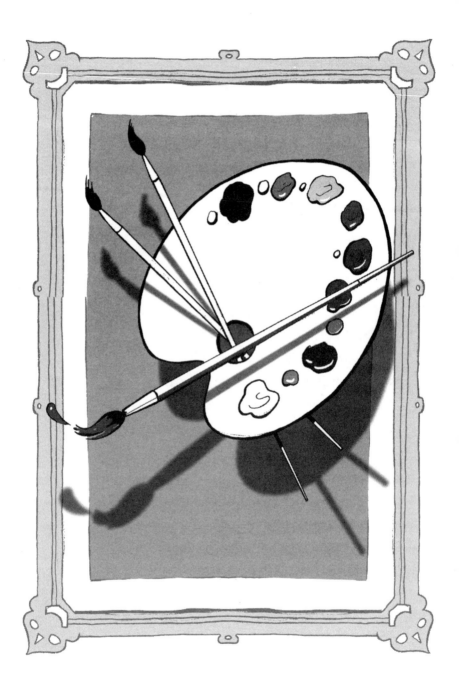

6

Secret Service

Sammy looked across the street at the large tree in the yard. He scratched his head. He *thought* he had seen someone there.

"Hey, Sammy, get busy!" Chris yelled from across the lawn. Sammy turned back to his work and soon had a large pile of leaves in front of him.

With all of them working, it didn't take long to rake the thousands of leaves into several large piles. Willie, Mr. Teller, Chris, DeeDee and Sammy filled a dozen large bags with the leaves. Then the kids carried them to the back of the pickup and tossed them in.

"Where are you taking these leaves, Mr. Teller?" Sammy asked.

"Willie's grandfather has a mulch pile that he uses to fertilize his garden each spring," Mr. Teller explained. "Some leaves have too much acid to make good mulch, but these will do just fine."

Sammy looked up to the porch and caught himself. He hardly recognized it! Not only had Maria, Jenny and Mrs. Wallace cleaned all the windows, they had swept the front porch floor and cleaned all the cobwebs off the beams above the porch.

"That looks fantastic!" Sammy said. "Mrs. Sheckly won't know it's her house!"

"Yeah," Jenny said, looking up and taking a deep breath. "I just wish we could repair the hole in the porch that I made here the other day."

"Hey guys, I think they're coming!" shouted Willie, whose wheelchair sat on the sidewalk. He stared down the long street.

Mr. Teller loaded the last bag into the pickup. "Good timing, kids. We're just finished. Let's quickly put the tools in the van. Then Mrs.

Wallace and I will move the van and truck."

"You kids can go hide in the bushes over there and see what happens," Mrs. Wallace said as she picked up her cleaning supplies and threw them into the back of the pickup.

Half a minute later, the van and pickup zoomed away, and the Shoebox Kids were safely hidden behind some bushes across the street. Willie had to duck down in his wheelchair to be hidden and yet be able to see.

"There they are!" Jenny whispered loudly. A blue station wagon pulled into Mrs. Sheckly's driveway and stopped. Mrs. Sheckly got out slowly from the passenger side. Jenny noticed that the neighbor who had driven Mrs. Sheckly was grinning as she got out of the car.

"She doesn't even notice!" Sammy said as Mrs. Sheckly walked across the lawn and onto the porch.

"We have to remember that she can't see very well!" Jenny whispered back. "She'll see it eventually."

As if in response to Jenny's comment, Mrs. Sheckly stopped at the top of the stairs, almost as if she had forgotten something. She looked around at the clean windows and the swept floor and ceiling. Then she turned and looked at the yard.

The Shoebox Kids began to giggle when they saw her looking around.

"Shh," Jenny urged them, but the giggling grew louder.

"I can almost hear her," Sammy said. "She's asking herself, *Is this my house?*"

"This is great," Chris added. "Better than a practical joke."

"Yeah, better because everybody wins," added Willie.

Sammy smiled and looked around at his friends, who were smiling too. Then he noticed that DeeDee wasn't smiling. She looked next door at the large tree where Sammy had looked earlier. A tall thin man stood in the shadows of the overgrown tree, staring at Mrs. Sheckly's house.

"That's the same man I saw coming out of the rosebush in her backyard," DeeDee said.

"Who is he?" Chris asked.

"I don't know," Sammy said. "But I have a feeling we're going to find out sooner or later."

The leaf-raking adventure was all the Shoebox Kids could talk about when they got together at church that weekend. After the lesson, Mrs. Shue gave them time to share their story. "That was so great," Chris said. "We've got to do it again."

"Yeah, maybe we could do the back yard next time," Willie added. "Of course, we'd need machetes and a jungle guide."

"And a big game hunter to look for snakes and tigers," added Sammy.

"I'm not going back there again," DeeDee said. "Not as long as that man is running around loose."

"What man?" asked Mrs. Shue.

DeeDee told her of the man she had seen coming out of the rosebush in Mrs. Sheckly's back yard, and of seeing him again beneath the tree across the street.

"I think that's the same man I saw at the art museum," said Sammy.

"Well, I think the police need to know that he's been hanging around," Mrs. Shue said. "I'll ask them to keep an eye out for him."

Jenny waited for Sammy in the hallway after the others had left.

"Who do you think that man is?" Jenny asked.

"Obviously someone who knows Mrs. Sheckly," Sammy said.

"If he's any danger to Mrs. Sheckly, then we need to do something," Jenny said.

"Mrs. Shue is telling the police," Sammy said. "But I want to know who he is."

Jenny took a deep breath. "I feel bad that we left that hole in her front porch. How about you and me going over there and fixing it tomorrow?"

Sammy thought for a minute, then nodded. "I can bring my grandfather's hammer and nails. We might not be able to patch it like a real carpenter would. But we can keep other people from falling in the hole too."

Jenny and Sammy got permission to go over early the next morning and try and patch the hole Jenny had left in the boards. Sammy took several short boards with him, as well as a hammer and nails.

The two of them crept onto the front porch as quietly as they could. Jenny carried the hammer and nails while Sammy balanced the boards. She watched as Sammy held one board against the hole, then another. All the time, he was mumbling to himself.

"What are you mumbling?" Jenny whispered.

"Grandfather wouldn't let me use his power saw. So I had to collect a bunch of boards and hope that one of them fits the hole you left here," Sammy pulled off a loose piece of flooring that stuck out at an angle.

Jenny didn't like the way Sammy had said that. "It wasn't my fault that I fell through the floor here," Jenny hissed. "Anyway, you didn't help things any."

"Well, you *told* me—" Sammy paused in mid-sentence as he found a board that fit the hole in the floor almost perfectly. "Got it!"

"Shh!" Jenny whispered. "We don't want to wake Mrs. Sheckly up. By the way, how are you going to nail that board down without waking Mrs. Sheckly up?"

"Remember she's hard of hearing," Sammy said.

"I have trouble *seeing*." Jenny and Sammy heard a familiar voice behind them. "I have ears like a bat."

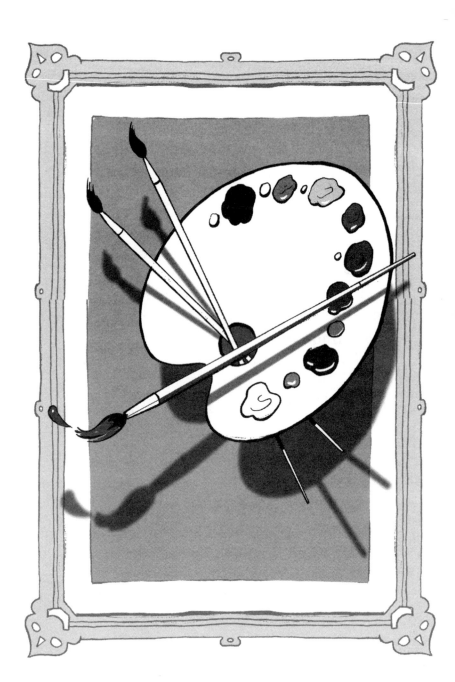

7

Caught!

"Just what do the two of you think you are doing?" Mrs. Sheckly asked, stepping toward Jenny and Sammy.

Jenny and Sammy stood suddenly, their backs to the hole they were trying to patch. Startled, Sammy was speechless, and Jenny felt her face burning.

"Oh, hi, Mrs. Sheckly," Jenny stammered.

Mrs. Sheckly stopped and looked at Jenny up and down. "You look like you've healed," she said. "How are you feeling?"

Jenny relaxed when Mrs. Sheckly changed

the subject. "I feel fine, thank you," Jenny said. "You told me to come back and visit you."

"And so you did," Mrs. Sheckly said. She bent her neck, trying to see what Jenny and Sammy hid behind them. "Now back to my original question: What are you two doing out here?"

Jenny and Sammy looked at each other, then shrugged. They stepped back so Mrs. Sheckly could see the boards, nails, hammer and hole in the porch floor.

"We—we—felt bad about the hole, so we wanted to come over here and fix it," Sammy said quietly.

"I told you not to worry about that old porch," Mrs. Sheckly said. "But if you felt so bad about it, why didn't you ask me first?"

"We wanted it to be a surprise," Jenny said.

Mrs. Sheckly paused and thought. "You were the ones who raked the leaves and cleaned the windows!"

Jenny and Sammy nodded. "With some friends," Sammy added.

"Why, you sweet dears," she said, more to herself than to Jenny and Sammy. "Just a minute, and I'll get my purse and pay you something for your work."

Caught!

Jenny held up her hands and shook her head. "No, no, please don't do that. We did it because the Shoebox Kids are Christians. Christians do good things for people. And we especially wanted to do something good for you."

Mrs. Sheckly backed up a step. "Me? Why me?"

Jenny took a deep breath. "Because you looked like you needed a few friends. And we wanted to be friends with you."

Sammy nodded. "Friends do things for each other."

Mrs. Sheckly blinked, and looked like she didn't know what to say. The three of them stood looking at each other. Suddenly, the silence was broken by a howl.

"Rowww!" The howl came from behind the two kids. Sammy jumped a foot in the air, and Jenny let out a squeak of fear.

"Oh kids, relax," Mrs. Sheckly said, shuffling forward in her house slippers. "It's just Dragon."

Dragon? Sammy mouthed to Jenny. "What's a dragon?" he said out loud.

"Dragon's just a silly old cat," Mrs. Sheckly said, reaching into the ivy behind them. She pulled out a huge yellow ball of fur and drew the

65

5—B.D.M.

cat to her chest.

"That must have been the cat we saw when we came here the first time," Jenny said.

"Dragon's been out all night, and I'm sure he's hungry," said Mrs. Sheckly. She looked up. "How about you two? Are you hungry? I can make some pancakes."

Jenny grinned at Sammy. Sammy grinned back. "Sure, why not. I think I have room for a couple of dozen."

In the kitchen, Mrs. Sheckly made pancakes in an old iron skillet on her antique stove while Dragon ate his breakfast in the corner on the floor. Sammy sat at the old table and looked around. Wallpaper curled off the walls in the corner. A yellowed calendar on another wall was dated "March, 1979." Bits of food lined the floor around the stove and refrigerator. He cringed. *I'm glad my house doesn't look like this*, he thought.

"You have a nice house," Jenny said. Sammy stared at her, but she continued. "I've always liked big old houses like this."

"Well, it's much too big for me to keep clean," Mrs. Sheckly admitted. "I have a hard enough time just taking care of myself and Dragon."

She looked around her, blinking behind her thick glasses. "But this is home for me. Always has been," she said brightly. "I was born upstairs, did you know that?"

Jenny shook her head, then shot a glance at Sammy.

"Mrs. Sheckly, what was your name before you got married?" Jenny asked cautiously.

Mrs. Sheckly put her spatula down by the frying pan and turned toward the kids.

"Why, don't you know?" she asked Jenny. "I'm Sheffield Matheson's oldest child, and his only daughter."

Sammy's eyes grew wide. "You knew Sheffield Matheson?"

Mrs. Sheckly chuckled. "I should say so. He was both father and mother to me after my mommy died. I got married young—a big mistake—and then divorced. I stayed away from home only about six months. The rest of my life I lived right here."

Jenny spoke up. "Mrs. Sheckly, you said that there was no painting. How do you know for sure?"

She chuckled again. "Oh, I know, believe me. The studio used to be right out there where the back yard is now. The only thing left is the cement slab that it was built on. Everything burned up."

Jenny frowned. "I'm not so sure. Can I look at your family Bible again?"

Mrs. Sheckly shrugged. "Sure. You know where it is. Daddy used to say it held all the treasure we needed. Do you think there are clues there?"

"Maybe," Jenny responded. She disappeared for a second into the living room, then returned with the big Bible.

"Were you here the night the studio burned?" Sammy asked.

Mrs. Sheckly nodded slowly. "That was a night I will never forget. I had gone to bed early. Daddy was working late in his studio, trying to finish the last of his Children's Dozen paintings."

"What they call the Broken Dozen now," Sammy interrupted.

Mrs. Sheckly nodded. "I woke up when I heard shouting and then a door slammed. Then I heard a motorcycle roar off. The only person I knew that had a motorcycle was Berkeley."

"That was your brother." Sammy added.

Mrs. Sheckly nodded again. "A few minutes

later, I smelled smoke and looked out the window. The studio was in flames! I called the fire department and raced down the stairs and outside to the studio. But by that time the fire ... and Daddy was ..."

Her voice choked off and paused. Sniffing, she turned away from Jenny and Sammy. "But that was a long time ago."

"What happened to Berkeley?" Jenny asked, and Sammy started getting an idea.

"He disappeared," Mrs. Sheckly said. "The police went to question him about the fire, but never found him. I haven't seen him since."

"That must be pretty hard, living all these years without your Mommy or Daddy—or brother."

Mrs. Sheckly looked out the window. "I wish I had a chance to talk to Berkeley," she said. "Daddy was always harder on him. But I don't think Berkeley started the fire. It wasn't like him."

Sammy cleared his throat. "Mrs. Sheckly, several times we've seen a man hanging around here, and once over at the museum." He went on to tell her what he and DeeDee had seen. "Could that be your brother?" he asked finally.

Mrs. Sheckly shrugged. "It could be. I haven't

seen him in over thirty years."

"Maybe you'll see him again," Jenny said.

"Maybe." Mrs. Sheckly paused. "I'd like that. I have so much to tell him—and ask him."

She flipped a couple of pancakes off the skillet and onto a waiting plate. Putting the plate in front of Sammy, she said, "Better eat these while they're hot."

Sammy didn't need further encouragement. He dug his fork into the steaming pancakes and stuffed them into his mouth.

Jenny shuddered. "Don't you want butter or syrup on them?" she asked.

Sammy shrugged. "Aw wak em amy ow way," he responded, his mouth crammed with pancake. He chewed for a moment, swallowed, then repeated himself. "I like them any old way." He grinned.

"You said you saw this man at the museum?" Mrs. Sheckly asked, placing more pancakes in front of Jenny.

"Sammy saw him," Jenny said, smearing butter on her pancake. "We were there at the Sheffield Matheson exhibit. I'm surprised that they didn't ask you to be there."

Mrs. Sheckly shrugged. "They asked me, but

I have too hard a time getting around. I probably couldn't see much of the art anyway. I'm pleased you kids take an interest in art."

Sammy shrugged. "They're planning on building a children's wing to the art museum. Jenny's mom is in charge of raising the money, and asked us to help raise it."

Jenny looked up at Mrs. Sheckly brightly. "Do you know any way the Shoebox Kids could raise money?"

Mrs. Sheckly frowned as she thought. "Are you interested in recycling things?"

Jenny nodded. "Sure."

"I have several years' worth of aluminum cans and newspapers in the garage," Mrs. Sheckly said. "For that matter, there could be a lot of things of value in there. I haven't been able to drive for years, so I haven't moved my car. Anything could be in there."

Mrs. Sheckly stepped forward and put her hands on Jenny and Sammy's shoulders. "Are you interested in cleaning out my garage in exchange for whatever treasures are in there?"

Jenny and Sammy looked at each other, and nodded. What treasures would they find in the old garage?

8

Dragon's Lair

Four phone calls and an hour later, the entire group of Shoebox Kids had invaded Mrs. Sheckly's yard. Mrs. Wallace and Mr. Teller had agreed to come with the pickup and van to haul off whatever trash—or treasures—they found. They held their breath as they waited for Mrs. Sheckly to open the big door to her garage.

"I haven't used these keys in years," Mrs. Sheckly said, as she fumbled through a large ring. "I'm not even sure the lock will work." She finally found a small round one more by feel than by sight. "Here it is," she muttered to herself.

"Jenny, can you help me here?" she finally asked. Jenny stepped forward and helped her get the key into the bottom of the fat padlock on the giant door. They wiggled the key for a long moment before the top of the padlock popped free and they were able to take the lock off.

Everyone gasped as they pushed the garage door open. A huge cloud of dust blew out from the open door, and several of the children began coughing. Then the dust cleared, and they could see inside.

"Wow," Willie said.

"That's a lot of newspapers," Chris said.

Sammy couldn't believe his eyes. From floor to ceiling, the garage was filled with stacks and stacks of newspapers. On one side, Sammy saw black plastic bags filled with something else. Chris poked one with his finger.

"Pop cans," he announced.

"I never throw anything away," Mrs. Sheckly said.

"I guess not," Sammy said.

"OK, kids," Mr. Teller said finally. "First, let's load these bags of cans into the pickup. Make sure the bottoms don't fall out of the bags. Some of them look pretty old."

Even with all the help, Sammy found himself making trip after trip from the garage to the pickup. Soon the back of the pickup was full, and there were still many bags of cans to be collected.

"Let's go ahead and fill up the van as well," Mr. Teller suggested. Mrs. Wallace and Mr. Teller switched the van and truck, and soon the van was being filled as well.

"Boy, Mrs. Sheckly," Chris said, sweat running down his face as he carried the last of the bags to the van. "You sure drank a lot of pop over the years."

Mrs. Sheckly smiled. "I have a weakness for grape soda," she said. "I didn't realize how big a weakness it was until today."

"That's the last bag!" Maria shouted.

"And that's all the room we have in the van!" responded Mr. Teller. "Mrs. Wallace and I will take these bags to the recycling center. You kids start bundling up the newspapers. We'll be back in a few minutes."

The Shoebox Kids watched the two vehicles drive off, then turned and looked at the stacks and stacks of newspapers. The stacks towered high over their heads.

"I'll bet some of these newspapers are pretty old," Willie said.

"Yeah, and the farther back you get, the older they would be," Maria said.

Chris just stared at the solid wall of newspapers. "There's supposed to be a car buried in there," he said, as if he didn't believe it himself.

"Over here, guys." They heard DeeDee's muffled voice off to the side. They followed it to a narrow alley between two high walls of newspaper. "I've found something—eek!"

"What is it?" Maria yelled back.

"Oh, yuck!" she said finally. "Something's dead back here!"

Sammy pushed his way through the narrow alley and found DeeDee in a back section that was more open. Feathers were scattered on the garage floor. Small bones and bits of fur were also there.

"Something killed some birds and maybe some mice here," Sammy said.

In response, a low meow came from above. Sammy and DeeDee looked up at the garage rafters. Sammy recognized two big yellow eyes.

"Dragon!" he scolded. "Shame on you!"

"Oh, come on," DeeDee said. "He's just being a cat. Our cat does the same thing. Come down here, Dragon, and make friends."

Dragon meowed again and hopped the short distance down from the rafter to the top of the newspaper piles. Soon the big yellow cat was nestled in DeeDee's arms.

"Hey guys, look at this!" Willie shouted, as Sammy and DeeDee pushed their way out of the alley and into fresh air again. Willie and the others were huddled around a corner of the garage, looking at the floor. Sammy and DeeDee pushed their way forward. Someone had scratched a date into the concrete floor.

"It says 1969," Chris said. "So what?"

"That means that the concrete for this garage was poured five years after the fire," explained Willie. "This garage wasn't here when the Matheson studio burned down."

Jenny spoke up. "Mrs. Sheckly said that the cement slab was still here from the studio. It must be somewhere else here in the back yard."

"Yeah, but where?" Maria asked.

"I'm not going back there," DeeDee said.

"I'm sure Dragon knows his way around

there real well," Sammy said. "He's the king of the jungle."

"Come on, guys," Maria said. "Back to work." She reached up and grabbed an armload of newspapers.

"Yeah, I want to see what kind of car could be hidden behind all these newspapers," Chris said.

"Where's Dragon?" DeeDee asked Sammy.

"You had him when we came out of his hiding place," Sammy answered. "Maybe he went back there."

"Or maybe he went looking for another mouse," Chris added.

"He'd better not," Sammy said.

"Dragon!" DeeDee called. She climbed back into the narrow alley to Dragon's lair, and called for him again.

"Come on, DeeDee, we've got work to do," Sammy said, taking a string and tying another bundle of newspapers together.

"Dragon's not in there!" DeeDee said, coming out of the alley. "He must have gone outside.

"Let him go, DeeDee," Sammy said.

"Hey, guys—guys—look at this!" Chris pulled down another stack of newspapers and motioned to the others to look. Behind the stack, Sammy and the others saw the shape of an automobile covered with a canvas.

"Wonder what kind it is?" Chris asked.

Suddenly there was a scream from outside.

Everyone looked at each other. "DeeDee," Sammy and Chris said at the same time.

"She probably saw another dead bird," Willie agreed.

Then they heard another scream. "Help! Help!"

Deep in the Earth

Sammy and the others ran out of the garage and looked into the overgrown back yard. DeeDee was nowhere in sight.

"Help me!" They heard DeeDee's voice again, but it sounded far away.

"DeeDee! Where are you?" Sammy yelled.

"I'm right here," she yelled back. "I fell down a hole!"

Mrs. Wallace and Mr. Teller drove up at that moment, and Chris and Maria ran to tell them what had happened.

Mrs. Wallace ran to the back yard, and Mr.

Teller went to his van to get a rope and a flashlight.

"DeeDee!" Mrs. Wallace called over the high weeds. "Are you all right?"

"I—I—I guess so," DeeDee said quietly. "It's just dark down here."

"Keep talking, DeeDee, and we'll find you," Mrs. Wallace said.

Mrs. Wallace, Mr. Teller, and the rest of the Shoebox Kids spread out at arms length from each other. As DeeDee kept calling, they slowly walked across the yard. Suddenly Maria stopped.

"I found her!" Maria shouted. She was in the far end of the back yard. As the others joined her, Maria pushed the high weeds away to show a hole about a foot across in the ground. Sammy could hear DeeDee's voice below them.

Mr. Teller lay down on his stomach beside the hole and called down to DeeDee.

"DeeDee, we're here now. Are you OK?"

"Yeah," she said, and Sammy noticed that she didn't seem to be as scared now. "I got wet when I fell in here. What is this place? It feels like it's made out of cement."

Mr. Teller shone his flashlight down at

DeeDee. Sure enough, Sammy could see her about ten feet below them, standing in the water up to her knees.

"It looks like some sort of old cistern," Mr. Teller said. "They used to use these to store water. The concrete on this one must have broken through here on the top." He shone his light around for DeeDee to see.

"Hold on, DeeDee," Mr. Teller said. "I'll tie a loop in our rope. You put it under your arms and we'll have you out of there in a jiffy."

"Wait," DeeDee said suddenly.

Why would DeeDee want to wait to get out of such a scary place? Sammy wondered.

"I think I see something down here," DeeDee said. "Mr. Teller, can I borrow your flashlight?"

Mr. Teller tied his large flashlight to the end of the rope and lowered it down so DeeDee could reach it. She grabbed it and took it loose. Then Sammy heard her slosh away from the hole where they huddled above her. After a long minute, she yelled back up to them.

"There's some sort of pipe sticking into the side of the cistern," she yelled. "And there's something loose inside of it."

"Pull it out," yelled Chris.

Sammy heard her twisting it and struggling below them.

"It's loose in there, but it won't come out. I can push it back in the pipe, but it drops back down."

Sammy wanted to jump down in the hole with her and find out what it was she was talking about.

"Describe it for us," Sammy finally shouted.

"It's metal, and it's round, like a tube," she shouted back. "But it has a cap on it. I think there's something in it!" She was silent for another long moment. Then Sammy saw her come back to the hole.

"Pull me up," she said. "I couldn't get it loose."

Mr. Teller lowered the rope again, and DeeDee put it under her arms. They pulled her up through the hole. When she got to the surface, Maria and Jenny hugged her.

"I've never been so glad to see the sun," DeeDee said. "And all of you!"

"We're glad to see you, too," Mrs. Wallace said. "You're sure you're all right?"

DeeDee nodded. "Just wet," she added.

Mrs. Wallace went to get towels and some

dry clothes for DeeDee, who was already telling everyone what she saw.

"It's like I said. I found a big pipe coming in from the side of the cistern."

"It must have been a fill pipe or vent of some sort," Mr. Teller said.

"Anyway, I saw something shiny sticking out of it," DeeDee continued. "I tried to pull it out, but it must be attached to a rope or chain on the other end."

"It fits!" Everyone turned around to see Jenny grinning and jumping up and down.

"What fits?" Sammy asked.

"The clues in the Bible!" Jenny pulled a piece of paper out of her back pocket. "Look," she said, pointing at her scribbled notes. "The family Bible opened to Micah 7:19, and I noticed that the word depths was underlined. Beside that verse were three others: Deuteronomy 5:8, Romans 15:20 and Revelation 20:1. When I looked those verses up, each one had a word underlined as well: *beneath*, *foundation*, and *chain*. Mr. Matheson was trying to tell his children where he hid his last painting!"

"Depths, beneath, foundation, chain—it's in the pipe!" DeeDee exclaimed. "But how did he get it in there?"

"Maybe that pipe comes out of the ground around here somewhere," Sammy said.

"Most likely, it comes out where the old studio used to stand," Mr. Teller said.

"But we've already looked around for the concrete slab and couldn't find it," Chris said. "We need someone who can tell us where it is."

"I know exactly where it is."

Sammy saw DeeDee turn and scream. When he turned, his mouth fell open.

In the driveway facing them stood Mrs. Sheckly and the mysterious gray-haired man.

The Missing Masterpiece

"Kids," began Mrs. Sheckly, "I would like to introduce you to Berkeley Matheson, my brother."

"Your brother!" Chris and Maria shouted at the same time. "Why he's—he's—."

"He's the man who came out of the rosebush and scared me!" DeeDee said.

"And stared at Sammy at the museum," Jenny added.

"And was watching Mrs. Sheckly's house from the across the street," said Sammy.

"Yes, yes, I know, and I apologize for frightening all of you," Mr. Matheson said quietly. "I have never been good with people—especially children. I didn't mean to scare you—any of you. It's just—I didn't know what to expect. I've been gone a very long time, and I wanted to know what was going on before I showed up. I was afraid Elizabeth would still blame me for what happened."

"Berkeley, I never blamed you," Mrs. Sheckly hugged Mr. Matheson's arm.

"Where have you been all this time?" Sammy asked.

"Father and I never saw eye to eye on anything. He always wanted more for me than I wanted for myself. The night of the fire, we had a big fight. I decided that I was leaving home for good. I got as far as the next big city, and changed my mind. I was ready to come home—until I saw the newspaper about the fire, and that the police thought I might have done it.

"I guess I panicked then. I traveled around on my own for a long time. I always wanted to come home, but I felt so guilty that I never could face the past or think of facing my sister.

"I've mostly worked at odd jobs all my life. One day last week, I read about the new exhibit featuring Father's work. I knew I had to see it, but I didn't want anyone to recognize me. When you," he pointed at Sammy, "waved at me at the museum, I was sure that everyone would recognize me for who I was—the son who killed Sheffield Matheson."

Berkeley looked at his sister. "It's not true, you know. Father was alive and well when I left."

Mrs. Sheckly looked up at Mr. Matheson. "I've always known you couldn't have done it."

"Then what caused the fire?" Sammy asked.

Mr. Matheson looked up. "Well, why don't we go find the studio's foundation? Maybe we can find the other end of that pipe. And just maybe there are answers there to some of our questions."

Mr. Matheson and Mrs. Sheckly walked back out to the driveway and the group followed. Mr. Matheson talked to Mrs. Sheckly as if he were trying to remember something.

"Let's see, the driveway used to curve around here," he gestured with his right hand at the ground. "And this garage wasn't here, so we used to park over here, right in front of the studio." He pointed to the overgrown area behind the garage.

"If that's the case, then the studio was right over there," Mr. Matheson pointed, and then headed for an area that seemed to have fewer weeds. Mrs. Sheckly, Mr. Teller, Mrs. Wallace, and the Shoebox Kids followed him as if they were part of a parade. Sammy watched Mr. Matheson push the tall weeds out of the way, and then motion for the others.

"See how the weeds are all really small here?" he asked the kids. "There's dirt here, but underneath it all," he pushed the loose dirt away to show hard concrete, "is the foundation for the old studio. Now if I'm guessing correctly, somewhere along the edge of this foundation, you will find something that looks like a pipe sticking up with a plug in it."

The Shoebox Kids scattered, and they all started looking for the pipe with the plug. Less than five minutes later, DeeDee let out a shout. "I found it!"

Everyone ran over to where DeeDee knelt on the concrete. She brushed away dead weeds and dirt, exposing a cast iron pipe that stuck out of the foundation at an angle.

"It will take a wrench to get that plug off,"

Mr. Teller said. "I'll get one out of the van."

The Shoebox Kids waited excitedly while Mr. Teller ran to the van and brought back a big wrench.

Mr. Teller placed the wrench on the square end of the pipe plug and began to twist. It didn't budge.

"It's been on there a long time," explained Mr. Matheson.

Mr. Teller tried again. Slowly, the metal plug began to turn in the cast iron pipe. The plug moved easier after a while. But Mr. Teller stopped before the plug had come completely off. He turned to the group.

"Since this is Jenny and Sammy's mystery, I think they should have the honor of taking the plug off."

"Yeah," shouted Chris and Willie.

Jenny and Sammy grinned at each other. Together they turned the wrench the last turn around. The plug fell out of the pipe, but hung suspended by a chain attached to the inside of the plug.

Jenny pulled on the plug, and Sammy grabbed the chain. Together, they pulled it further and further out of the pipe.

"I see something!" Chris shouted. Sure enough, a silver tube started to come out of the pipe. It was just as DeeDee had described it. It had a metal cap on it, but it was about three inches wide and a couple of feet long.

"Open it!" they all shouted as the tube came completely out of the pipe.

Sammy held the tube and Jenny carefully unscrewed the cap. The cap came off and she looked in the tube.

"I see something on canvas in here," she said, grinning. She looked at Mrs. Wallace. "Mom, is it safe to take it out?"

Mrs. Wallace shook her head. "It's been in there for thirty years, sweetheart. I'm sure he protected it properly, but I would suggest we let professionals take it out at the museum."

"And that's just where it belongs," said Mrs. Sheckly. "In the museum with the rest of the paintings."

"Wait, there's an envelope in here too," Jenny said, reaching into the tube. "It's addressed to Elizabeth and Berkeley." She handed the envelope to Mrs. Sheckly and Mr. Matheson. They looked at each other and opened the letter. Mr. Matheson read:

Dear Children:

I leave this final painting for the two of you. It celebrates the joy of being a child, just as my other paintings do. Share it with the world. But remember, it belongs to you.

It is all I can give you. I realize that my heart is not as strong as it once was, and I do not have many days left to paint and be with the two of you. I'm sorry I kept my sickness from you.

Berkeley, I'm sorry I have been so hard on you. I only wanted the best for you. I have learned one thing through the years that remains true: family comes first. Be good to each other. Father

"He must have had a heart attack after I left him," said Berkeley. "Maybe the fire was started when he fell and knocked over a lamp or heater."

"If only we would have found this letter thirty years ago," Mrs. Sheckly said. "Think of the difference it would have made in our lives."

"So is the painting still going to the museum?" Jenny asked.

Mrs. Sheckly looked down at her. "You bet! It belongs with the exhibit—Daddy would have wanted that."

Mrs. Wallace smiled. "I'm sure the museum would be glad to return it to you when the exhibit is over."

Sammy Tan looked at the quilt spread out on the green grass, and the children huddled over their picnic. The watermelon looked juicy enough to eat, and the corn on the cob made his mouth water. *This Sheffield Matheson painting is the best one yet*, he thought. He looked around the exhibit hall at the other paintings. *And it seems to fit in perfectly.*

"Hey Sam-*mule*!" Jenny yelled from across the exhibit hall.

"What do you want, Jenny Wallflower?" Sammy yelled back.

Jenny came skipping over. "Did you hear? We made almost $500 from the cans and newspapers we've collected from Mrs. Sheckly and her neighbors. Five hundred dollars! I'm thinking of going into business!"

"Big deal," Sammy said. "Grandpa and I are helping Mr. Matheson get Mrs. Sheckly's old car running again. It's a '57 Chevy! Mr. Matheson says that when we get it fixed up and cleaned up real nice, we'll auction it off. Do you realize how much a car like that will earn for the children's wing?"

"Oh, it's just an old car. How boring!" Jenny said. She turned and looked at the painting of the picnic in front of them. "It sure is beautiful," she said.

Sammy nodded. "I still can't figure out why he called it Number 11 if they're supposed to each represent a month of the year. The eleventh month is November. Who would go on a picnic in November?"

Jenny shrugged. "Probably only Sheffield Matheson could answer that. I guess it's one mystery we'll never solve."